JONNY ZUCKER began his career in radio and is now a writer
and primary school teacher. Along the way he has played in
several bands and has worked as a stand-up comedian. Jonny has
written two books for adults: *A Class Act* and *Dream Decoder*.
He lives in London with his wife and their young son.

JAN BARGER COHEN, originally from Arkansas in the U.S.A.,
is a well-established illustrator of children's books.
Her previous titles include *Bible Stories for the Very Young*,
the Little Animals series, *Incy Wincy Moo-Cow, Who Can Fly?*,
Who Can Jump?, Who Eats This? and *Who Lives Here?*.
She lives in East Sussex with her husband
and a cocker spaniel called Tosca.

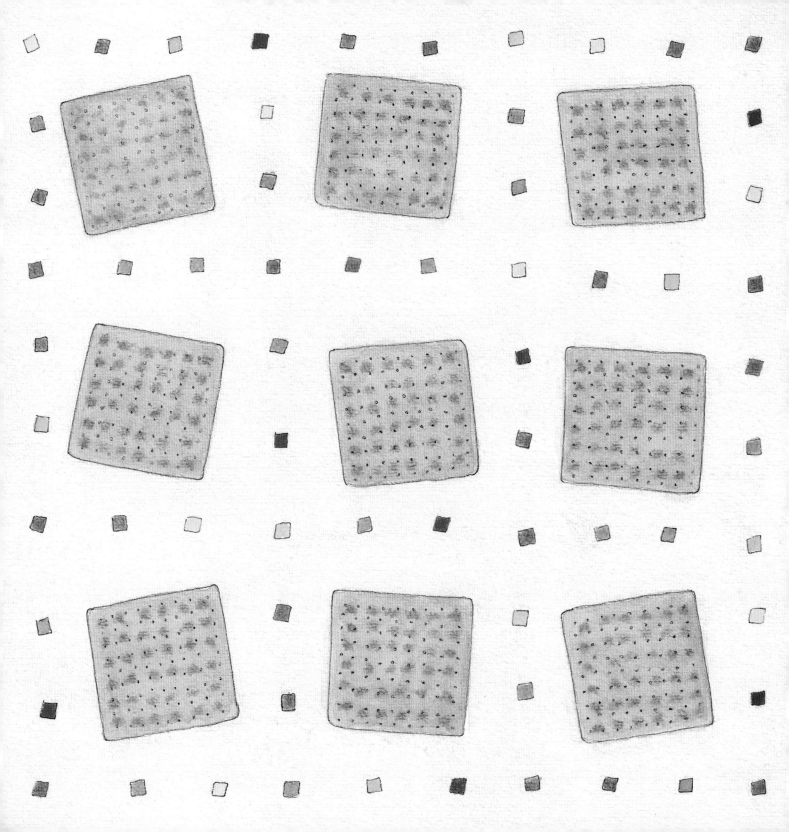

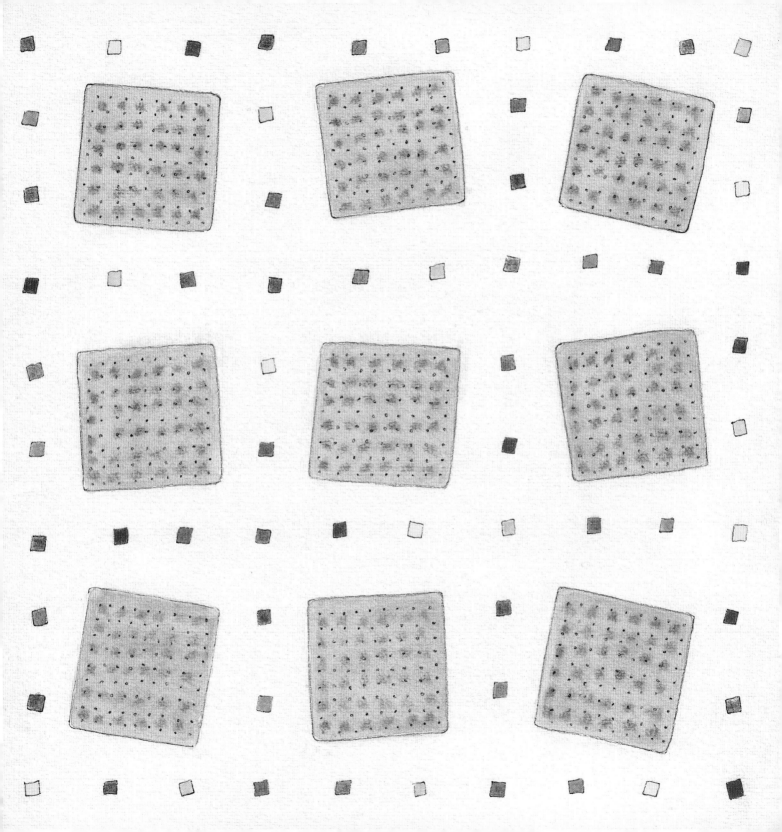

For Talia and Joseph – J.Z.
To Geoffrey and Audrey – J.B.C.

Four Special Questions copyright © Frances Lincoln Limited 2003
Text copyright © Jonny Zucker 2003
Illustrations copyright © Jan Barger Cohen 2003

First published in Great Britain in 2003 by
Frances Lincoln Limited, 4 Torriano Mews,
Torriano Avenue, London NW5 2RZ

www.franceslincoln.com

First paperback edition 2004

British Library Cataloguing in Publication Data available on request

ISBN 0-7112-2018-2

Printed in Singapore

3 5 7 9 8 6 4 2

The Publishers would like to thank Bryan Reuben for checking the text and illustrations.

FESTIVAL TIME!

Four Special Questions

A Passover Story

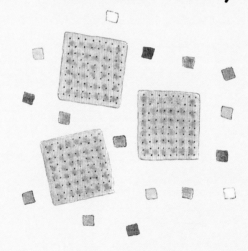

Jonny Zucker

Illustrated by Jan Barger Cohen

FRANCES LINCOLN

Passover is here and we remember how our people were once slaves in Egypt. I'm sweeping up all the breadcrumbs with a feather.

For eight days we're going to eat matzah, just like the Children of Israel did when they escaped from Egypt.

It's time for the Seder. I like to see the Seder plate with the six different types of food.

My brother asks four special questions about why this night is so different from other nights. I will be old enough to ask them next year.

We hear about ten plagues that God sent to the Egyptians.

River into Blood

Frogs

Boils

Hail

Lice

Flies

Death of Beasts

Locusts

Darkness

Death of the First Born

Dad hides the Afikoman – a special half piece of matzah – and we all search for it. I find it first, but we all get a present!

We sing songs about the past and the future to celebrate our festival of freedom.

What is Passover about?

Many years ago, Pharaoh, the ruler of Egypt made the Jews work as slaves. Moses, the leader of the Jews, went to Pharaoh and said, "Let my people go!". But Pharaoh refused.

So one night, God told the Jews to escape from the land of Egypt under the cover of darkness. As they fled, they didn't have time to bake their bread properly, so they had to take it with them before it leavened. This unleavened bread is called **matzah**, and we eat it today at Passover to remind us of the escape from Egypt.

At Passover time, we search our homes for **chametz** – pieces of bread, or crumbs. When we find them, we throw them away or burn them.

We celebrate Passover by having a **Seder** service. This means 'order'. It is a time for everyone to hear the story and to talk about the time of slavery and the escape from Egypt.

The story is retold in a special book called the **Haggadah**.

On the Seder table, three matzot are placed on top of each other, and the middle one is broken in half, and one half (the **Afikoman**) is hidden. Later in the evening the children need to find the Afikoman. The one who finds it gets a prize.

There is a special Seder plate. On this there is a bone to remind us of the paschal lamb of Egyptian times; an egg, which is a symbol of new life; a bowl of **charoset** which is a mixture of apples, nuts and wine, to remember the bricks the Jewish slaves were forced to make; two lots of bitter herbs, which remind us of the bitter time the Jews had as slaves and the **karpas** (a vegetable – normally parsley) which is dipped in salt water as a reminder of the tears shed by the Jews.

During the Seder, the youngest child who is able asks four questions about why this night is different from other nights. Four cups of wine are drunk during the evening, and a special cup is reserved for the prophet Elijah.

Before and after the Seder meal, everyone sings songs, to bring joy to the evening and to remind us that once we were slaves, but now we are free.

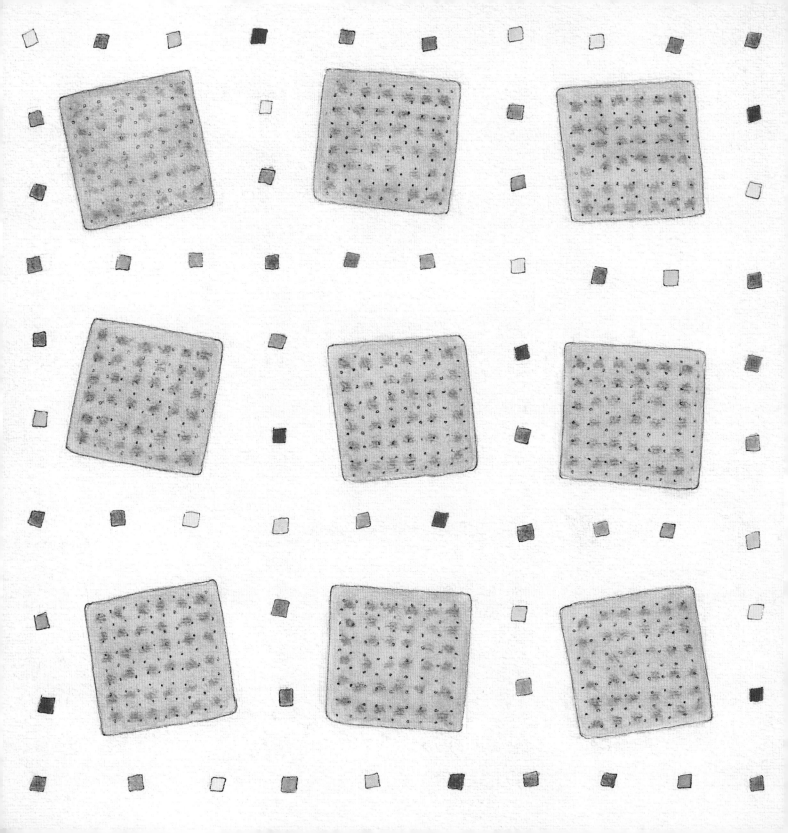

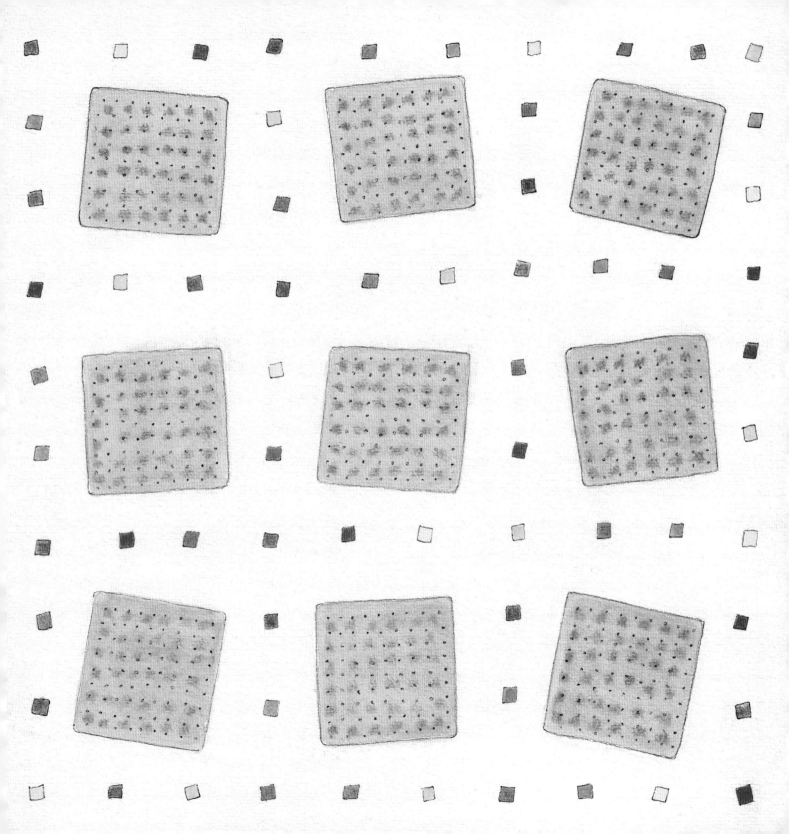

MORE TITLES IN THE FESTIVAL TIME! SERIES BY JONNY ZUCKER AND JAN BARGER COHEN

Apples and Honey – A Rosh Hashanah Story
See how a Jewish family celebrates New Year,
eating apples and honey and hearing
the sounds of the Shofar.
ISBN 0-7112-2016-6

Eight Candles to Light – A Chanukah Story
Follow a family as they light the menorah,
open presents and eat latkes.
ISBN 0-7112-2017-4

It's Party Time! – A Purim Story
A story about how a family celebrates Purim:
dressing up in costume, giving presents
and making lots of noise!
ISBN 0-7112-2019-0

Frances Lincoln titles are available from all good bookshops.
You can also buy books and find out more about your favourite titles,
authors and illustrators on our website: www.franceslincoln.com